DANA DOESN'T LIKE GUNS ANYMORE

Written by Carole Webb Moore-Slater
Illustrated by Leslie Morales

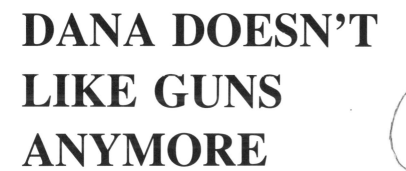
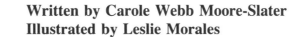

Friendship Press
New York

GUNS ARE NOT HEALTHY for CHILDREN or OTHER LIVING THINGS

BillDay

Join with other concerned citizens and take a pledge of personal disarmament:

I will not carry, keep or own a handgun.

The continuing handgun murders, especially of our children, convince me that having a handgun actually increases the risk of injury or death for me and my family. I urge others, especially the young, to join me in this important step in our effort to help stop this terrible slaughter.

Art by Bill Day from gun control poster of the Anti-Handgun Association, Detroit, Michigan. Art used courtesy of the Coalition to Stop Gun Violence, 100 Maryland Avenue, N.E., Washington, D.C. 20002; (202) 544-7190

FOR SARAH AND DANA

Copyright © 1987 Carole Moore-Slater
This revised edition 1992 Carole Moore-Slater
FRIENDSHIP PRESS

Editorial Offices:
475 Riverside Drive, New York, NY 10115

Distribution Offices:
P.O. Box 37844, Cincinnati, OH 45222-0844

Manufactured in the United States of America

LIBRARY OF CONGRESS

Moore-Slater, Carole Webb.
    Dana doesn't like guns anymore / written by Carole Webb Moore
-Slater ; illustrated by Leslie Morales.
        p. cm.
    Summary: Dana learns that guns are dangerous when he plays with a friend's BB gun and a tragedy occurs.
        ISBN 0-337-00246-1 : $10.95
        [1. Firearms —Fiction. 2. Safety—Fiction.] I. Morales, Leslie
ill. II. Title.
PZ&. M788157Dan 1991
[E]—dc20

                                                                91-033403
                                                                CIP
                                                                AC

Special Thanks to Mom, Jim, Pat, Linda, Leslie and Corinne for inspiration to make this book possible.

T his is a story of a boy named Dana
and a bird called Meadowlark.
Dana and the Meadowlark lived
together peacefully in the country where the
green grass grows tall and the skies are blue.
The Meadowlark was a beautiful bird with a
bright yellow belly and striped wings that
often perched on a branch in the big pine tree
outside Dana's bedroom window.

Each morning, the Meadowlark would greet the sun with a melody of songs, and each morning Dana would wake to sweet music in the air.

His mom told him that the song of the Meadowlark sounded like it was whistling *"Spring is sweet to me"* – which made Dana quick to jump out of bed when the Meadowlark came to call. He liked knowing that his favorite bird was a happy one.

Dana was a tall boy for his age with blond hair that wrinkled in front and curious blue eyes. He stood out in a group, not because he was too tall, but because he always wore a bright red baseball cap on his head and cowboy boots on his feet. Dana was a rather serious boy about baseball, bicycling, and animals. He enjoyed them all very much. He was also very interested in toy guns although he did not have one.

Dana shared his big yard happily with the Meadowlark; Honey-bear, the big yellow dog; a gray fat cat named Kittyfur; and two snow white bunnies, Lilly and Willy.

Dana was kind to animals. He understood that animals had feelings too, so he tried to be a good friend and not tease, or hit, or be mean to his dog, cat, and bunnies. And so when Dana went outside in the yard, his animal family would playfully run with him, or fetch his ball, or just stand beside him to be petted.

Even the bunnies like to play and would often chase Kittyfur or Honeybear around in circles – which made Dana and his sister Sarah laugh and laugh. Dana was glad that the dog liked the cat and the cat liked the bunnies and the bunnies liked Kittyfur and Honeybear. The Meadowlark also seemed to know that Dana was a special friend to animals because it spent long hours in Dana's yard splashing in the bird bath and singing in the trees.

When Dana was not playing with his animal friends, he was playing with the boys and girls who lived nearby. Sometimes Dana would dig tunnels in the sand with Pat and Lisa, or play baseball in the backyard with Michael, Jayne, and his dad, or ride his bicycle up and down the driveway with Sarah.

But there were times when the boys met at the woods by the edge of the yard to play soldier games. Pat had a laser gun, Michael used a cowboy gun, but Dana did not have a gun at all. Not one gun. Dana could not have a gun because his mom and dad said that guns only hurt people and animals.

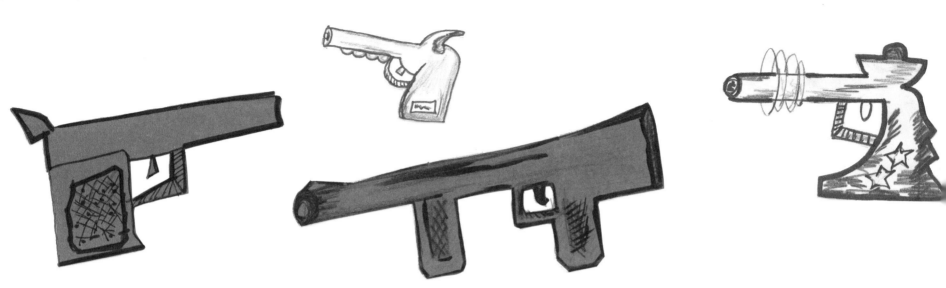

Dana wished he had a special gun just like his friends. He thought, "If guns are so bad, why do so many people have them on television....and why are there so many guns in the toy store?"

Dana remembered all the guns he had seen in the toy store – there were big guns, little guns, loud guns, quiet guns, space guns, war guns, dart guns, cap guns, pop guns, green guns, black guns, rubber guns, metal guns and squirt guns.

Dana could not understand why he could not have a toy gun of his own. It was just not fair – guns were **FUN!**

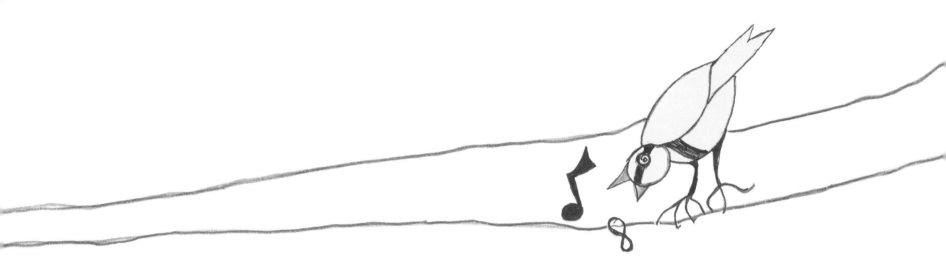

One warm spring day, Dana went next door to visit his older friend Jeff. On the way, he stopped to watch a meadowlark sail through the sky and perch on a nearby telephone line. The Meadowlark's song sounded sweeter and louder than ever before and Dana wished he understood bird talk because he was sure that bird was talking to him.

Jeff was in the side yard, shooting his new BB gun that he got for his birthday. Dana's eyes got big as he watched Jeff with his gun. Dana really wanted to hold the gun but he knew that his mom and dad would not like it.

Just the night before, his parents told him again that guns were dangerous, and because they did not think it was right to shoot birds, bunnies, or any other animals, no gun of any kind was allowed in the house…and that included toy guns. No guns at all was the family rule.

About that time, Jeff looked at Dana and asked him if he wanted to shoot the gun. Dana's heart started beating fast as he slowly held out his hand toward the gun. He was excited-but scared – what would his parents do if they found out?

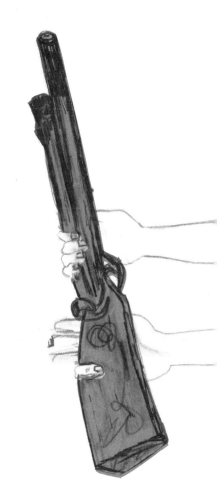

ana looked at the gun
hard as he carefully
turned it over and over in his
hands. It was a brand new,
shiny gun with a long, black
barrel and silver trigger.
It shined in the sunlight.
Dana slowly aimed the
gun into the sky and pulled
the trigger. BANG went the gun
as the BB flashed through the air.
Dana felt just like GI Joe!!!
He thought that his mother
and father did not know how
much fun it was to really
shoot a gun!

Dana's arms relaxed as he aimed the gun into
the sky again. It was a beautiful day!
The sky was bright blue and fluffy white
clouds softly moved along each time the wind
blew. With a smile on his face, Dana aimed
at the clouds. BANG went the gun again.

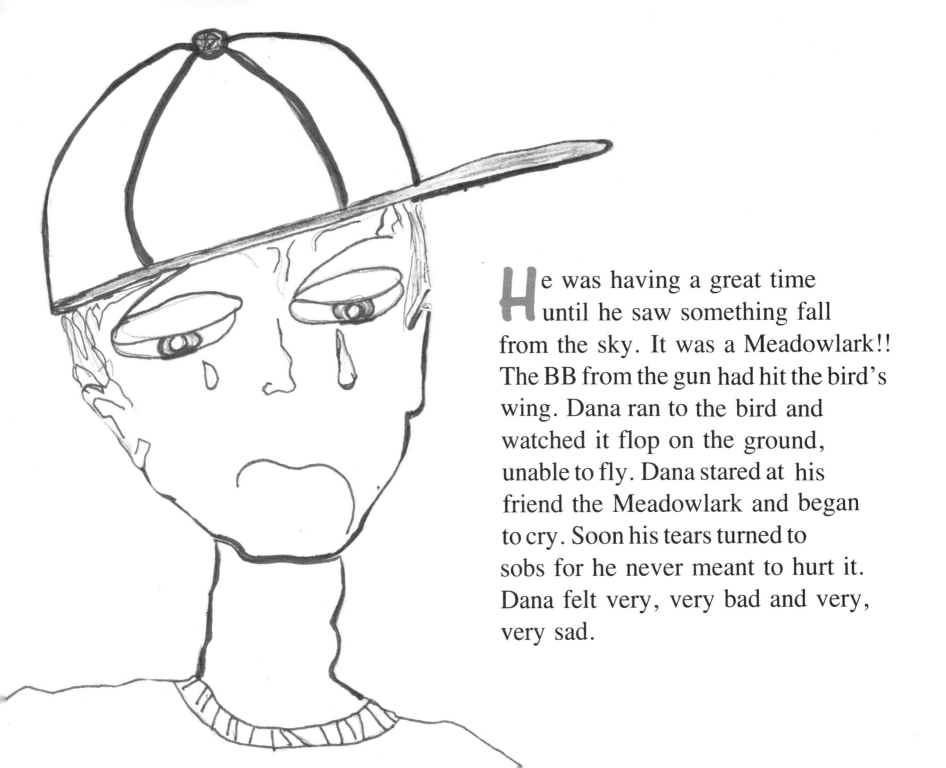

He was having a great time until he saw something fall from the sky. It was a Meadowlark!! The BB from the gun had hit the bird's wing. Dana ran to the bird and watched it flop on the ground, unable to fly. Dana stared at his friend the Meadowlark and began to cry. Soon his tears turned to sobs for he never meant to hurt it. Dana felt very, very bad and very, very sad.

Dana's dad heard his cries and went outside. There by the big pine tree stood Dana with tears running down his cheeks as he sadly looked at the wounded bird. The brand new shiny BB gun lay on the ground beside his feet.

Dana helped his dad gently wrap the Meadowlark in an old towel while his mom called a friend who takes care of injured birds. The ride to see Wren Hill was a long one for Dana.

Wren Hill looked at the bird's wing and knew just what to do. She carefully bandaged the Meadowlark's wing. Dana was asked to prepare the cage with soft dry grass and fresh water. Helping the injured bird made Dana feel better.

The Meadowlark did not die. But Dana has changed. He no longer asks his mom and dad for a gun of his own... Dana doesn't like guns anymore.